HENRY

JAMES

PERCY

First published 1992 by Buzz Books
an imprint of Reed Children's Books
Michelin House, 81 Fulham Road, London SW3 6RB
and Auckland, Melbourne, Singapore and Toronto

Reprinted 1993

Copyright © William Heinemann Ltd 1992

All publishing rights: William Heinemann Ltd
All television and merchandising rights licensed by
William Heinemann Ltd to Britt Allcroft (Thomas) Ltd
exclusively, worldwide

Photographs © Britt Allcroft (Thomas) Ltd 1985, 1986
Photographs by David Mitton and Terry Permane
for Britt Allcroft's production of Thomas the Tank
Engine and Friends

ISBN 185591 209 0

Printed and bound in Great Britain by
BPCC Hazell Books, Paulton and Aylesbury

WOOLLY BEAR

buzz books

It was summer and Percy had returned from being mended after his accident with the trucks.

At this time of year the gangers cut the long grass along the side of the line. They rake it into heaps beside the line to dry in the sun.

When Percy comes back from the
harbour, he stops where they have been
cutting. The men load up his empty wagons
with hay, and he pulls the wagons to the
station.

8

Toby then takes them to the hills for the farmers to feed their animals.

"Wheeeeeeesh!" Percy gave a ghostly whistle. He was teasing Thomas about the time when Thomas had thought he had seen Percy's ghost. "Don't be frightened, Thomas," Percy laughed. "It's only me!"

10

"Your ugly fizz is enough to frighten anyone," said Thomas. "You're like . . ."

"Ugly indeed! I'm –"

"– A green caterpillar with red stripes," continued Thomas firmly. "You crawl like one too."

"I don't," said Percy.

"Who's been late every afternoon this week?" asked Thomas.

"It's the hay," answered Percy.

"I can't help that," said Thomas. "Time's time, and the Fat Controller relies on me to keep it. I can't if you crawl in the hay till all hours."

"Green caterpillar indeed!" fumed Percy as he set off to collect his trucks to take to the harbour.

"Everyone says I'm handsome – or at least *nearly* everyone," said Percy. "Anyway, my curves are better than Thomas's corners."

Percy ran along with his trucks and spent the morning shunting. "Thomas says I'm always late," he grumbled. "I'm *never* late – or at least only a few minutes. What's that to Thomas? He can always catch up time further on."

All the same, Percy and his driver decided to start home early.

Then came trouble.
CRASH! A crate of
treacle was upset all
over Percy. They wiped
the worst off but he
was still sticky when
he puffed away.

18

The wind rose as they travelled along and soon it was blowing a gale.

"Look at that!" exclaimed the driver.

The wind caught the piled hay, tossing it up and over the track. The gangers tried to clear it but more always came.

Soon they came to a place where the line climbed higher. "Take a run at it, Percy," his driver advised.

Percy gathered speed. But the hay made the rails slippery, and his wheels wouldn't grip. Time after time he stalled with spinning wheels, and had to wait till the line ahead was cleared before he could start again.

Everyone was waiting. Thomas seethed impatiently.

"Ten minutes late! I warned him. Passengers'll complain, and the Fat Controller . . ." he muttered.

The signalman shouted, the station
master stood amazed and the passengers
laughed as Percy approached.

"Sorry I'm late!" he panted.

"Look what's crawled out of the hay!" teased Thomas.

"What's wrong?" asked Percy.

"Talk about hairy caterpillars!" puffed Thomas. "It's worth being late just to have seen you!"

When Percy got home, his driver showed him what he looked like in a mirror.

"Bust my buffers!" exclaimed Percy. "No wonder they all laughed. I'm just like a woolly bear! Please clean me up before Toby comes."

But it was no good. Thomas told Toby all about it and instead of talking about sensible things like playing ghosts, Thomas and Toby made jokes about 'woolly bear' caterpillars and other creatures that crawl about in hay.

They laughed a lot, but Percy thought
that they were really being very silly
indeed.

THOMAS

EDWARD

GORDON